The Hero's Quest

Jeffrey Alan Love

WALKER STUDIO
AN IMPRINT OF WALKER BOOKS

For Gwyneth,
Arthur &
Owain

First published 2019 by Walker Studio, an imprint of Walker Books Ltd, 87 Vauxhall Walk, London SE11 5HJ • © 2019 Jeffrey Alan Love • The right of Jeffrey Alan Love to be identified as author/illustrator of this work has been asserted by him in accordance with the Copyright, Designs and Patents Act 1988 • This book has been typeset in Historical Fell Type Roman • Printed in China • All rights reserved. No part of this book may be reproduced, transmitted or stored in an information retrieval system in any form or by any means, graphic, electronic or mechanical, including photocopying, taping and recording, without prior written permission from the publisher. • British Library Cataloguing in Publication Data: a catalogue record for this book is available from the British Library • ISBN 978-1-4063-8788-9 • 10 9 8 7 6 5 4 3 2 1

WWW.WALKERSTUDIO.COM

This story begins, as all stories must,

With a rider appearing
from out of the dust;

Called to the quest by the
Ancient One's cries,

A hero who stands
beneath towering skies;

A rider
who dares
to charge
against
fate

Past dragons
that gather,
to watch and
to wait

And elves in the night with swords wreathed in flames

To caverns where dwarves play their hidden games;

Beneath gods in their clouds,
their mountains, their trees,

Where kings
and queens rule,
just as they please;

Across lakes that lie silent,
keeping secrets so deep,

Waking creatures of magic,
of wishes, of sleep;

Swearing oaths in the night, solemnly sealed,

A ravening wolfpack
chasing at heel;

Through places unknown,
edge-of-map lands,

To a tower of stone where the Ancient One stands

With a new
quest for *you*,
a hero we
trust:

And the story
begins again,
as all stories
must.